Little Dorrit

Written by **Charles Dickens**
Illustrations by **Alessandro Valdrighi**

스푼북

Welcome to Marshalsea

A long time ago, there was a prison in London called Marshalsea. It was a horrible, dark and dingy place, close to the River Thames.

Anyone who borrowed money but could not pay it back was thrown into Marshalsea. They were not released until their debts were paid. But, you see, once a person was locked inside Marshalsea, they could not earn any

money. So, they could not pay their debts, and they had to stay in prison.

Some prisoners stayed there for years and years. Children were born and families were raised inside the mouldy walls of Marshalsea.

One such family was the Dorrits. There was Mr William Dorrit, his wife, Mrs Dorrit, their son and their two daughters. The Dorrits had always been very poor. To get by, Mr Dorrit had borrowed money – money which he could not pay back. Eventually, he owed so much money that two burly police officers marched up to the door of the Dorrits' tiny run-down house and arrested him. Mrs Dorrit held tight to her children and wept as they followed Mr Dorrit into Marshalsea prison.

Our story starts more than twenty years after that fateful day. By this time, Mr Dorrit's wife had sadly died, their children had grown into adults and he had made the prison his home. He had a small room, with two or three bits of furniture, and plenty of friends. The other prisoners called him the Father of the Marshalsea – a title he was very proud of.

Visitors were introduced to Mr Dorrit and new prisoners were welcomed by him. It was as if he were the master of a grand household rather than an old man,

locked in a prison cell.

Of his three children, Mr Dorrit was closest to his daughter, Amy. People often called Amy Little Dorrit, partly because she was the youngest and partly because she was very small. She lived alone in a room just outside the prison walls, so that she could be close to her father.

Mrs Clennam's Horrid House

Amy Dorrit earnt a small wage by sewing and doing other small tasks for a woman called Mrs Clennam. She was a hard-faced lady, with tiny silver spectacles. Behind those spectacles sat her cold grey eyes, which matched the steely shade of her hair.

Though Mrs Clennam lived in a large house with plenty of rooms, she would often tell Amy that she had not left her bedroom for many years. 'Twelve whole years!' she would croak. 'I could not possibly leave this room. I'm too ill.'

Then she would cough and splutter, as if to prove her point.

Just as Mr Dorrit almost enjoyed being locked in prison, Mrs Clennam seemed to enjoy being ill.

One day, Mrs Clennam's son, Arthur, came home. He had been living in China for a long time, looking after the business which his father owned. But now that his father – Mrs Clennam's husband – had died, Arthur had returned to England.

Mrs Clennam had not got on with her husband. She didn't get on with her son either. In fact, Mrs Clennam didn't get on with anyone.

'I hope you are well, Mother,' said Arthur as he stepped into her room and peered at the cobweb-covered walls.

'I shall never be well again,' she snapped.

Mrs Clennam did not hug her son or kiss his cheek, even though she had not seen him for many years. She barely mustered a smile.

Delving his hand deep into his pocket, Arthur pulled out a small wooden box and handed it to his mother.

He was careful not to brush her bony fingers as he did so. It was a pocket watch that had belonged to his father. His father told him very clearly that when he died, Arthur should give this watch to his mother.

Mrs Clennam opened the wooden box and drew in a shaky breath. Sat on top of the watch was a small circle of silk, with the words: "Do not forget" stitched onto it.

Arthur watched as his mother raised the scrap of silk to her grey eyes and read the message.

'What does it mean, Mother?' he asked. 'What should you not forget?'

'Nothing,' she spat, waving him away with her hand. 'It's nothing to do with you.'

Arthur looked round his mother's room. It was dark and gloomy, and smelt faintly of mould. There was a table in one corner and in the other ... a girl. How had he not seen her before?

She was sitting on a chair, sewing.

'Who are you?' Arthur asked.

'That is Amy Dorrit,' his mother said. 'I pay her to do sewing and cleaning and other such things – things that are of no business to you, Arthur.'

Arthur was even more surprised. His mother already had a couple of servants. Why would she employ somebody new? She would not give someone a job out of the kindness of her heart. She had no kindness in her heart.

Arthur Clennam stayed at his mother's that night. He slept in his old bedroom at the top of the house. The whole place was so ugly and grim now that he could not think of it as his home.

There were piles of dust everywhere. The windows were so dirty you could hardly see in or out

of them, and the windowsills were sprinkled with dead bugs.

The house creaked and groaned as though it might fall apart at any moment.

Arthur slept badly. He wondered what his father's message meant: "Do not forget". He wondered whether his family had a deep, dark secret. Had they done something wrong in the past?

It was no good asking his mother. Mrs Clennam would never admit to doing anything wrong. Only other people did things wrong.

The next morning, Arthur saw Amy Dorrit again. She was a shy girl, but not quite as young as she had first seemed. She had hazel eyes, but she hardly dared to lift them from the floor.

She was so shy, in fact, that she ate her meals by herself at Mrs Clennam's house.

Arthur became curious about Amy. Who was she? And where did she come from? He decided to find out.

A Visitor at Marshalsea

One evening, when Amy Dorrit left the Clennams' house, Arthur followed her. He kept his distance as the little figure slipped through the busy

streets.

Eventually, she came to an old red-brick building near the River Thames. She knocked at a dirty wooden door that had iron bars at the top. A face appeared behind the bars. Beady eyes peered through at Amy before the door was unlocked and she

slipped through.

Arthur waited a moment. Then he walked up to the same door and knocked.

Again, a man's face appeared behind the bars.

'What is this place?' asked Arthur.

'It's Marshalsea prison, sir,' said the man. His name was Bob; he was a guard at the prison.

'Can anyone go in here?'

'Anyone can go *in*,' said Bob. 'But not everyone can come *out*.'

'Is there a person called Dorrit in here?'

'Mr Dorrit? Oh yes. He is the Father of the Marshalsea. Would you like to see him?'

Arthur nodded and Bob unlocked the door to let him in. They walked across a small courtyard and up a flight

of narrow stairs to Mr Dorrit's room.

Standing in the doorway, he saw Amy Dorrit preparing her father's supper. It was the dinner that she had been given at Mrs Clennam's house. Arthur suddenly realised that this was why she ate her meals alone: she never really ate them at all! She packed them away and fed them to her father.

When Amy turned and saw Arthur, her cheeks flushed a deep red.

Arthur cleared his throat. 'Mr Dorrit, it's a pleasure to meet you. I'm Arthur Clennam. Amy works

for my mother.'

Mr Dorrit did not blush. He simply welcomed Arthur in and offered him a chair. He told Arthur all about the prison, and how he was known as the

Father of the Marshalsea. He said that visitors often gave the Father of the Mashalsea a little “offering”.

By “offering” he meant money.

Before Arthur could say or do anything, a young woman burst into the room. It was Mr Dorrit’s elder daughter, Fanny.

Fanny Dorrit was a dancer, that was plain to see. As well as being pretty, she walked with her head held high and her feet barely touching the ground – as if she were floating on a cloud.

‘Have you mended that dress of mine, Amy?’ Fanny Dorrit asked her

sister.

Amy handed her the mended dress. Fanny took it without even a "thank you" and marched back out the room. The moment Fanny closed the door of her father's cell, a loud bell rang. It was a signal for all visitors to leave the prison – or else they would be shut in for the night.

Quickly, Arthur Clennam slipped some coins into Mr Dorrit's outstretched hand. Amy looked up and her cheeks grew even redder. She hated to see her father begging for money. But Arthur simply said his goodbyes and left the room.

He was walking across the courtyard when Amy caught up with him.

'I'm so sorry, sir,' she said. 'I'm sorry that my father was asking for money like that.'

'No, Miss Dorrit,' said Arthur. 'It is *I* who am sorry. You must forgive me for following you here. I had no right to barge into your family life.'

The two talked for a few minutes about Amy's life at Marshalsea, Arthur's life in China and the strange habits of mean Mrs Clennam, which made them both giggle.

They were so lost in their conversation that they didn't notice the bell had stopped ringing.

Oh dear! Now the front gate was locked and Arthur and Amy could

not leave.

They would have to spend the night in Marshalsea prison.

Mr Pancks Investigates

Arthur had never spent a night in prison. He certainly did not enjoy it, but it wasn't *terrible*. He got to spend a little longer with Amy Dorrit, and he was very curious about her and her family.

He wondered why his mother liked Little Dorrit. Mrs Clennam was such a mean old woman, so rude and unkind to everyone else, including him. Did it have something to do with the message in the watch box?

Arthur had to know. So when he left the prison the next day, he went to see a man named Pancks, who liked to think he was a detective. Arthur asked him to find out more about the Dorrits.

Mr Pancks was a short, stubby man, who was always out of breath. He was always busy, though nobody knew what he did.

‘Do you know what I call myself, Mr Clennam?’ said Mr Pancks.

‘No,’ said Arthur.

‘I call myself a “fortune teller”,’ said Mr Pancks. ‘It’s not because I tell the future. It’s because I go out looking for fortunes. Fortunes which people might have lost or never even known about.’

During Mr Pancks’s strange investigation, Arthur grew very close to Amy Dorrit – they became the best of friends. He also happened to meet a man called Daniel Doyce. Daniel was an inventor and an engineer.

He owned a tiny factory. And though his workspace was small, his ideas were huge, imaginative, and even groundbreaking. Arthur was amazed.

'You are a genius, Daniel Doyce,' he said as Daniel explained the function of each cog, wheel and pin in his latest invention. 'Why don't we work together? You supply the ideas and I'll supply the money.'

Daniel barely thought for a second before he shouted, 'Yes! Absolutely yes!'

And so, they set to work creating their new company: Doyce & Clennam.

Just for a moment, everything seemed to be going well.

While Arthur was working and Mr Pancks was "investigating", Amy's sister, Fanny Dorrit, was flirting as usual.

Lots of people fought for Fanny Dorrit's heart. One of them was Edmund Sparkler, a rather foolish young man, from a rather foolish family.

Edmund's mother was the wife of Mr Merdle, who was very rich. He made his fortune by encouraging people to put their money into his bank.

Edmund's mother, Mrs Merdle, had a very high opinion of herself. She had a rich husband. She had a rich son. She was part of *society*.

Being part of *society* meant certain rules had to be obeyed.

There were people you could be friends with. They were part of *society*. And there were people you could not be friends with. They were not part of *society*.

Mrs Merdle soon found out about the father of the girl Edmund was so fond of. He was most certainly *not* part of Mrs Merdle's society. This Mr Dorrit was a prisoner in Marshalsea, of all places! The news shocked her so much, Mrs Merdle nearly fainted. Her son could not, and would not, marry the daughter of a prisoner.

Without a moment's delay, Mrs Merdle invited – well, demanded really – Fanny Dorrit to visit her grand London house. Fanny asked Amy to join her. Together, they

walked through the huge door of Mrs Merdle's mansion, sat on her plush maroon chairs and gulped at the sight of the old woman as she strode into the room.

'Fanny Dorrit,' said Mrs Merdle, 'I will not waste any time with chit-chat. You cannot see Edmund ever again.'

Fanny's face changed quickly from shock to anger.

'Fine,' she said. 'I don't want anything to do with *him* anyway.'

'Then we are agreed,' said Mrs Merdle, slipping something into Fanny's hand.

When they were stood outside the heavy door of the grand house, after it had been swiftly slammed behind them, Amy asked Fanny what Mrs Merdle had given her. Fanny opened her hand to reveal a tight roll of banknotes.

'Oh Fanny,' said Amy. 'You should not have taken her money.'

'You little fool,' said Fanny. 'Haven't you got any self-respect? If that lady insults me, then she will pay for it. And she has paid, see.'

But Amy Dorrit saw things differently. In her eyes, her sister *lost* self-respect by accepting money in this way. It was just like her father taking "offerings" from his visitors.

From Rags to Riches

Not long after the trip to Mrs Merdle's, the Dorrits received some rather exciting news. It seemed that suddenly their troubles were over.

Mr Pancks, the man who Arthur asked to investigate the Dorrits, had made a discovery. He had found that there was once a family called Dorrit, who lived in a great house in Dorset. But the last Dorrit of Dorset had died. It seemed there was no one left to inherit the great house and all the land and money that went with it. No one, that is, apart from Mr William Dorrit.

The Father of the Marshalsea was rich!

He quickly paid off his debts and took one last look around his small, dirty cell before leaving Marshalsea prison forever.

Naturally, his family shared in his new riches.

Dressed in beautiful new bonnets, dresses and gloves, Fanny and Amy joined their father and brother in the carriage that drove them far away from Marshalsea, and far away from London.

Arthur Clennam waved them goodbye. He was glad to have helped the family escape the shadow of the prison, but he had to admit that he would miss his friend, his Little Dorrit.

A Gentleman in Venice

Mr Dorrit had not been beyond the prison walls for more than twenty years. He had not seen the rolling fields, the great, looming buildings or the bright sunshine of the outside world for a long, long time.

But Mr Dorrit was a gentleman now. He had money. He had a house in Dorset. He had a position to keep up. And above all, he was part of *society*.

The first thing Mr Dorrit did was put all his new money into Mr Merdle's bank. After all, everyone

said that Mr Merdle was brilliant with money. He kept it safe and the longer you had money in the bank, the more of it you made.

Arthur Clennam also decided to put his money into Mr Merdle's bank. He wanted to make more money for his business with Daniel Doyce.

Even Mr Pancks put money into Mr Merdle's bank.

Everyone thought Merdle was a money-making magician – they trusted him with every penny they owned.

The Dorrit family loved Dorset, but it still was not enough for them. Being part of *society* now meant that they could travel anywhere in the world. And so they did. They packed their bags and set off across Europe. They travelled across France, through the mountains of Switzerland and on to Italy.

Finally, they arrived in the remarkable streets of Venice. Sunlight glittered on the canals and the walls of the buildings glowed white, pink and gold.

Amy Dorrit had never been anywhere like Venice before, where rivers replaced roads and people travelled in boats rather than carriages. She described every detail

to Arthur in her letters, which he was always pleased to receive.

The Dorrits rented one of the finest mansions in Venice, which sat on the Grand Canal. They ate the best food. They met the best people. They went to see the most famous paintings and musical concerts.

Mr Dorrit even hired a woman to teach Amy and Fanny how to behave like *real* ladies. Mrs General was the teacher's name. She had a very boring voice and very boring rules.

'Do not say "father", say "papa",' she would snap at Amy. 'And do not roll your eyes, Fanny Dorrit. You are a lady now.'

Fanny Dorrit thought that being part of *society* would change their lives for the better. But, truly, she was a bit bored. She didn't really want to look at paintings or go to musical concerts. Sometimes she missed her days dancing in the theatre.

One afternoon, while Fanny was staring out of the window, picking at her skirt and feeling utterly bored, there was a knock at the door. To her surprise, Edmund Sparkler walked into the room. The same Edmund Sparkler whose mother, Mrs Merdle, had paid Fanny to go away.

But that was when Fanny Dorrit was the daughter of a poor man, a prisoner in Marshalsea. Now Fanny was the daughter of a very rich man.

In fact, a man who was rich enough to put a lot of money into Mr Merdle's bank.

Mrs Merdle had no objection to Fanny now. Not now that she was part of *society*.

And in that room, on that late afternoon in Venice, Edmund asked Fanny to marry him. Fanny

didn't really love Edmund, but she accepted anyway.

Amy Dorrit was not pleased at all. She knew that Edmund was not good enough for Fanny, and she knew that Fanny didn't love him. But Fanny just laughed.

'Oh, Amy,' she said. 'One day you will understand: marriage is not about love. It's about money.'

It seemed that Mr Dorrit agreed. He was pleased that Fanny was marrying Edmund. For him, it was a way of telling the whole world that the Dorrit family was now part of *society*.

At an absurdly large and extremely expensive wedding, Fanny Dorrit became Mrs Sparkler.

Mr and Mrs Sparkler then travelled back to London. They were going to live in Mrs Merdle's grand house, while his mother stayed in Venice.

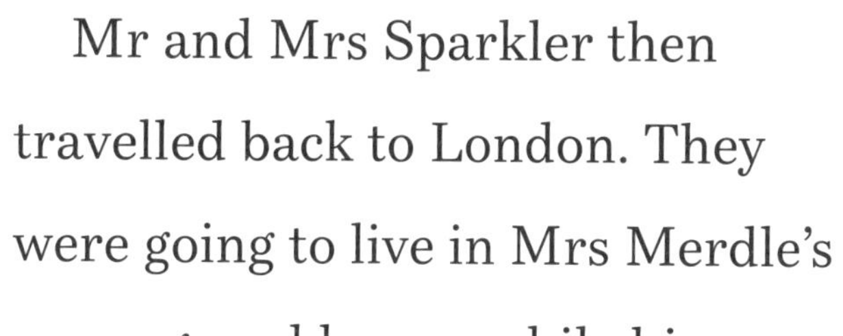

Mr Dorrit and Amy also stayed in Venice, soaking up the city and the sunshine. While Amy's brother travelled to Sicily and then to Naples, and enjoyed every penny of their new wealth.

The End of Mr Dorrit

Mr Dorrit seemed to grow very old very quickly. He shuffled about like an aged tortoise.

His memory became very bad. Sometimes he even forgot where he was. When he looked around, he didn't see the glittering canals of Venice. In his mind, he saw the red-brick walls of Marshalsea prison. And sometimes, when he was speaking to a servant, he imagined to was talking to one of the prison guards.

Amy tried to help him remember things, but it seemed that his mind was slipping away, like sand through her fingers.

The day came when, after many magnificent concerts and lavish balls,

Mrs Merdle decided to leave Venice. She threw a great dinner party to celebrate her time in the city.

Of course, Mr Dorrit and Amy were invited.

As the father and daughter came to the foot of the great marble staircase leading up to Mrs Merdle's dining room, Mr Dorrit stopped.

'Amy, my dear,' he said, 'send for Bob. He can help me up the stairs.'

Amy sighed. Bob was the guard at Marshalsea prison.

She knew her father's mind was slipping further and further away.

With Amy's help, Mr Dorrit climbed slowly up the marble stairs.

At the top, he turned and spoke to the guests who were just arriving downstairs. He welcomed them as if they were guests at Marshalsea.

By now, everyone was watching old Mr Dorrit with a mix of amazement and disgust.

He rambled on and on about being the Father of the Marshalsea. He even said that he would be pleased to accept any "offerings". The other guests shuddered and turned away, but Amy was not ashamed of her father. She put her arms round him and led him back downstairs.

They returned to their mansion on the Grand Canal. Amy made her father a warm drink and helped him into bed.

She stayed up all night, watching the old man drift in and out of sleep.

She held his wrinkled hand and talked quietly to him, whispering stories of their time at Marshalsea. Finally, Mr Dorrit closed his eyes for the last time.

Back in Mouldy Marshalsea

Back in London, something strange was happening to Mrs Clennam's house. It had started to creak and crack more loudly than usual.

Then, tiles began to fall like rain from the roof. The chimney lurched in the wind, and then crashed to the ground in a great cloud of dust. The dirty windows shattered to pieces. The floors upstairs shivered and quivered and tilted.

Finally, the whole place fell down like a pack of cards.

Sadly, Mrs Clennam was inside when it happened.

Arthur was sorry to learn of his mother's death, though she was never kind to him. He was not sorry, however, to see the house destroyed.

Only one thing had been saved from the disaster: a small, wooden box, full of letters. One of them was from his mother. It read:

To my dear Arthur,

When you read this, I will be gone and it will be time for you to learn of the secrets I have been keeping. I am not your real mother. Your father fell in love with a singer before we were married. Together, they had a baby: you. Your father's family did not approve. He was forced to leave her and marry me, instead.

Your real mother died soon after we took you from her. Your father's family felt it was partly their fault. So, in guilt, they left all their riches to the only person who truly cared for her, her patron, Mr Frederick Dorrit.

I hid this will and kept the riches for myself, and for you.

I am truly sorry.

Arthur sank to his knees. The Dorrits could have been rich all along. His dear Amy would never have had to grow up in a place like Marshalsea prison.

Unfortunately, Mrs Clennam was not the only person hiding a dark secret. It turned out that for many years, Mr Merdle had been cheating all the people who had put their money into his bank. He did not care for the money, or help it grow. He stole it.

And, eventually, he ran out of people to steal from.

Rather than face imprisonment, Mr Merdle simply disappeared. He left his house one night and was never seen again.

Everybody who had put their money in Mr Merdle's bank was now penniless.

The Dorrits lost their fortune. Amy and Fanny had nothing.

Mr Pancks lost his earnings.

Arthur Clennam lost the money for his business.

Arthur was most upset about letting down his business partner, Daniel Doyce. Daniel, however, was a kind and forgiving man. He did not blame Arthur for trusting Mr Merdle. But the law did not forgive as easily. Because of his debts, poor Arthur was locked away in the stinking cells of Marshalsea prison.

He was imprisoned in the very same room where Mr Dorrit had lived for more than twenty years.

After a few weeks in the cold, mould-filled prison room, Arthur fell very ill. He spent his days sleeping on the hard, narrow bed, coughing and sweating and drifting in and out of sleep.

One morning he awoke, his mind still dazed from sleep and illness, and was sure he saw someone else in the little room.

It was Amy Dorrit!

She was holding a cup of water to his lips and smiling at him.

'You helped us when were here in Marshalsea,' she said. 'Now I am here to help you.'

Arthur's smile was tinged with sadness. He thought of his mother's letter – he could not keep it from Amy.

He pulled the crumpled piece of paper out from under his bed and showed it to her.

When she had finished reading, Arthur said to her, 'Can you forgive us, Amy?'

'Us?'

'The Clennam family, I mean. It is our fault that your father and your family were locked away, here, in Marshalsea.'

'It is not *your* fault,' said Amy.

Tears welled in her eyes. She wiped them away with the back of her hand. Then she stood up, walked over to the tiny fire in the corner and threw the letter in.

'I have no money now,' she said. 'Like you, my family lost everything to Mr Merdle's bank. But you and I, Arthur, we still have each other.'

Arthur realised then and there that he loved Amy, just as she had always loved him.

Fortunately, Daniel Doyce still had a little money left and what he didn't have, he earnt. He paid Arthur's debts, freed him from prison, and asked him to keep working with him on their business. They would never be rich, but they would be happy.

They would be especially happy, since a few weeks after Arthur's release from prison, he and Amy were married. He would never have to say goodbye to his Little Dorrit again.

Charles Dickens

Charles Dickens was born in Portsmouth in 1812. Like many of the characters he wrote about, his family were poor and his childhood was difficult. As an adult, he became known around the world for his books. He is remembered as one of the most important writers of his time.

Alessandro Valdrighi

Alessandro Valdrighi studied stage design in Florence, Italy, where he received his bachelor's degree. Since he was a child, he loved to draw and drew after cartoons and illustrations for various books. Thanks to that, he was able to learn different styles of painting and enjoy new challenges. He works as a cartoonist, illustrator, and concept artist, and won the 2011 Best Comic Book Award in Spain.

LITTLE DORRIT

초판 1쇄 발행 2023년 6월 27일

글 찰스 디킨스 | 그림 알레산드로 발드리히

ISBN 979-11-6581-435-9 (74840)
ISBN 979-11-6581-418-2 (세트)

* 잘못 만들어진 책은 구입하신 곳에서 바꾸어 드립니다.

발행처 주식회사 스푼북 | 발행인 박상희 | 총괄 김남원
편집 김선영 · 박선정 · 김선혜 · 권새미 | 디자인 조혜진 · 김광휘 | 마케팅 손준연 · 이성호 · 구혜지
출판신고 2016년 11월 15일 제2017-000267호
주소 (03993) 서울시 마포구 월드컵북로 6길 88-7 ky21빌딩 2층
전화 02-6357-0050(편집) 02-6357-0051(마케팅)
팩스 02-6357-0052 | 전자우편 book@spoonbook.co.kr

제품명 Little Dorrit
제조자명 주식회사 스푼북 | **제조국명** 대한민국 | **전화번호** 02-6357-0050
주소 (03993) 서울시 마포구 월드컵북로6길 88-7 ky21빌딩 2층
제조년월 2023년 6월 27일 | **사용연령** 8세 이상
※ KC마크는 이 제품이 공통안전기준에 적합하였음을 의미합니다.

⚠주 의
아이들이 모서리에 다치지 않게 주의하세요.